P9-CCP-013

A FRIBBLE MOUSE LIBRARY MYSTERY

The Secrets of the Rock

Phyllis J. Perry

Illustrations by Ron Lipking

UpstartBooks

Fort Atkinson, Wisconsin

**For Casey, Clare, Julia, Emily, and Kenny,
who are all good friends of Fribble Mouse!**

Published by UpstartBooks
W5527 Highway 106
P.O. Box 800
Fort Atkinson, Wisconsin 53538-0800
1-800-448-4887

Copyright © 2004 by Phyllis J. Perry
Cover and interior illustrations by Ron Lipking

The paper used in this publication meets the minimum requirements of American
National Standard for Information Science — Permanence of Paper for Printed
Library Material. ANSI/NISO Z39.48.

"Look out!" Fribble Mouse squeaked, dropping his rake. He gave his best friend Tweek a violent push that sent them both head over heels into a leaf pile. A large rock rolled harmlessly past and came to rest at a flat spot beneath a nearby tree.

"Whew!" Tweek said, scrambling to his feet. "Gee, thanks, Fribble. I didn't see that big rock coming. It would have smashed me flat for sure."

Fribble got to his feet, too. His long tail swished through the air, and he stroked his whiskers nervously. "Close call," he agreed.

Their third grade teacher, Mrs. Tremble, had heard Fribble's shout, and she came charging up the hill. At the same time, their worried classmates came running down from where they'd been digging to make sure Fribble and Tweek were okay. Mrs. Tremble was a stout, middle-aged gray mouse, and she was puffing by the time she reached them. "Are you all right?" she asked Fribble and Tweek.

"We're fine," Fribble assured her and his classmates.

Mrs. Tremble examined each of them, from the tips of their noses to their long tails, to be sure they really weren't hurt.

All of the pupils in Mrs. Tremble's third grade class at Twitch Elementary School were at Pioneer Park this beautiful autumn afternoon. Each class in the school had volunteered to do a service project to help the community of Cheddarville in some way. Their class had decided to clean up this old park on the west side of town very close to where Fribble lived. In fact, Fribble and his little brother Scamper often came to Pioneer Park to play. They usually stayed in the sunny, open area close to Swiss Street where all the playground equipment was located.

On the hill at the upper end of the park were trees, flower beds, and a few picnic tables. Occasionally, Fribble had noticed an old mouse up there, sitting in the sun and reading a newspaper. But that part of the park was usually empty except for summer holidays when families came for picnics. Although Fribble and Scamper never went to that area, apparently quite a few others did. A lot of trash was scattered about, and weeds had completely taken over the flower beds.

Some teams of students, wearing work gloves over their paws, were filling trash bags with old bottles and papers. Other teams were pulling weeds and raking leaves. Fribble had volunteered for leaf patrol. He loved the gorgeous yellow, red, and brown leaves scattered deep over the ground like a fancy carpet.

Mrs. Tremble, relieved that no one was hurt, blew the whistle on the cord around her neck. She shouted, "Finish up what you're doing in the next ten minutes and meet at the park gate. It's almost time to walk back to school."

Everyone scurried about, taking their bags of trash to the big barrels standing outside the park restrooms.

But instead of running for the gate, Fribble and Tweek walked over to the rock for a closer look.

"Wow! It's almost as big as me," Tweek said, eyeing it up close.

Fribble slowly walked around it. "Sure is," he agreed. "You know, I don't think this is an ordinary rock. Look here." He pointed to what looked like bits of gray cement clinging to one whole side of the speckled granite rock. "It looks like it was cemented down some place. Like a statue or something."

Fribble continued to walk slowly around the boulder. He spotted something on the far side of the rock. "Hey!" he said, his whiskers twitching and his tail lashing through the air. "There's something on this rock." As he studied the rock, Fribble sniffed the air. He could smell dirt and mold.

"What do you mean?" asked Tweek. He ran around the rock to join Fribble.

Fribble pointed to an old marker that was securely fastened to the rock. It was square and looked like it was made of brass. But right now it was discolored and impossible to read. Fribble rubbed at the marker with his sleeve, but it was covered in dirt, moss, and grit. It was going to take serious work to get that marker clean again. Fribble couldn't read much of what was written there. But by scratching some of the dirt away, he could make out one word—"memorial." Fribble pulled out the little notebook and stubby pencil that he always kept in his back pocket, and carefully copied the word "memorial" into it.

"C'mon," Fribble said. "Let's look at the spot where the rock came from."

Fribble and Tweek ran up to where the students had been working when they'd accidentally dislodged the rock and sent it rolling down the hill.

"There's nothing here," Tweek said, looking around.

Fribble had to agree that there was nothing unusual, just a damp, flattened spot where the rock had rested in the dirt. But his gaze moved further up the hill, and he started scrambling higher. Tweek looked down toward Swiss Street to where their classmates were beginning to gather by the gate. "Hey, Fribble! It's time to go," he cried, then he turned and started back.

But Fribble continued up the hill—he was a very curious mouse. Suddenly, he spied what he'd been searching for. He found a cement base, resting beneath an old oak tree. Nothing was on the base now except for some jagged cement. That's where the rock with the marker was, Fribble thought to himself. I'll bet it was broken off a long time ago. Maybe some kids did it for mischief. And I'll bet it's been sitting halfway down the hill for years, until it got knocked farther down today.

As Fribble stood wondering about his find, Tweek called again. "C'mon, Fribble. It's time to go back to school."

Reluctantly, Fribble left the cement base and went running down the hill to join his classmates. He was quiet and thoughtful on the way back to class. He kept wondering about the marker. What did it say under all that dirt? What was it doing in Pioneer Park? The dismissal bell rang soon after they got to school, and Fribble left class still wondering about the rock.

Fribble met Scamper outside of his first grade classroom, and the two walked home together. Scamper chattered away about his day, and how his class was measuring and weighing pumpkins in math. Fribble half-listened and didn't say much. He was lost in his thoughts.

Once home, Fribble and Scamper dropped their backpacks and went to the kitchen for a quick snack of celery sticks and cream cheese.

"Mom," Fribble announced after he had finished crunching and munching, "I need to go to the library for a few minutes. Okay?"

"Can I go, too?" Scamper quickly cut in.

"Of course, you may," their mother said. "But don't stay long. I want you to get your homework done tonight, so your weekend will be free, because ..."

"We won't be long," Fribble broke in without waiting for his mother to finish her sentence. He grabbed Scamper's paw and hurried out the door.

It was only a short walk to the library, and on the way, Fribble told Scamper about the big rock in the park and the marker that was attached to it. They soon reached the steps of the library and hurried inside.

Miss Scurry, the librarian, greeted them. "Hi, I'm glad to see you two. Could I help you with anything today?"

"No, thanks. I just need to use your dictionary," Fribble explained, "and I know where it is."

He led Scamper straight to the dictionary, carefully carried the big book over, and set it on the library table. He pulled his small notepad out of his pocket and looked at the word he had copied down from the marker on the rock. "'Memorial' will be under 'M' and somewhere near the middle of the dictionary," Fribble explained to Scamper.

Fribble opened the book and began to turn the pages, looking at the guide words at the top of each page as Miss Scurry had taught him. He soon located the words "memorandum" and "mercy" at the top of a page. "It's between those two words, so it's somewhere in here," Fribble said, excitement in his voice.

He ran his finger down to "memorial" and read aloud to Scamper, "Anything, as a monument, intended to preserve the memory of a person or event."

"I don't get it," Scamper admitted.

"Hmmm," Fribble said thoughtfully, as he closed the dictionary. "It means that the marker on the big rock in the park is in memory of some important person or some important thing that happened. I wonder who or what it was?"

"How are we going to find out?" asked Scamper.

"We have to clean that marker so we can read it," Fribble said.

When Fribble and Scamper got home from the library, their mother asked, "Did you find what you were looking for?"

"Yes," Fribble said. He told her about the big rock in Pioneer Park and the marker covered in dirt that had the word "memorial" on it.

"Very interesting," his mother said.

"We're going to get that marker sparkly clean," Scamper said, "so we can read the rest of what it says."

"That sounds like a good idea, but not today," their mother said. "Fribble needs to do his homework. I want you to get it all done tonight, Fribble, because we're going to be busy this weekend."

"What's up?" asked Fribble, nose twitching.

"The two of you went running out of here so fast to go to the library that I never got a chance to tell you the good news. Great Aunt Squeegee is coming to visit us. She's arriving tomorrow and is going to stay for Thanksgiving."

"Hurrah!" shouted Fribble. Of all his aunts, Great Aunt Squeegee was his favorite. Instead of gossiping hour after hour with the grown-ups, Great Aunt Squeegee spent time with Fribble. She used interesting, big words, and she always asked him to help her with crossword puzzles.

On hearing the news, Scamper did a little dance. Fribble knew that Scamper loved tea parties, and Great Aunt Squeegee loved to drink tea. She always had time for tea with Fribble and Scamper, and she didn't care how many lumps of sugar they added. She was also a wonderful cook. Fribble knew that he and Scamper could count on some extra special goodies to eat in the days to come.

Fribble went straight to his room and did his homework quickly. He was so busy solving math problems and thinking about Great Aunt Squeegee, that he forgot about the marker on the rock.

That night, as Fribble fell asleep, he imagined how happy this Thanksgiving would be. His father traveled a lot for work, but he'd be home for Thanksgiving week. They'd be sure to see Grandma and Grandpa. And now Great Aunt Squeegee would be here, too.

As promised, Great Aunt Squeegee drove down from Apple City in time to be with them for lunch on Saturday. She was tiny but filled with energy. She almost bounced out of the car to come and squeeze each of them. After taking her suitcase up to the guest room, they all gathered around the dining room table to eat and catch up on everything that had happened since their last visit.

When everyone ran out of family news, Scamper told Great Aunt Squeegee about the Harvest Fair at school. He explained that everyone would want to go. There would be booths to visit and a cakewalk.

"The cakewalk's my favorite," Scamper said. "I won last year, and I bet I win again this year. 'Cause I'm very lucky," he explained.

"You'll come to the festival, won't you?" Fribble asked.

"Of course, I will," Great Aunt Squeegee said. "Wouldn't miss it. In fact, if you'd like, I could make a cake to take to the cakewalk."

Scamper beamed, and Fribble smiled at him. If his lucky little brother won again this year, Fribble knew which cake he'd pick!

Then Fribble told the story of the rock that rolled down the hill in Pioneer Park. Great Aunt Squeegee was immediately interested. "I wonder what that marker is in memory of?" she asked. "You must be dying of curiosity, Fribble."

"I am," Fribble admitted.

"We've got to clean it before we can read it," Scamper said.

"Well," said Great Aunt Squeegee, "after we help your mother with the dishes here, why don't we take some sudsy water and a scrubbing brush and go to the park?"

"Really?" Fribble squeaked. "You want to go?"

"Now, Fribble," Fribble's mother interrupted. "Your aunt must be tired after her drive. You certainly don't need to insist that she go traipsing over to the park to clean a dirty, old rock today. She may want to take a rest."

"I'm not the least bit tired," Great Aunt Squeegee insisted. "In fact, I'm a little stiff from sitting around so much. First sitting in the car and then here at the table. A walk to the park is just what I need."

So they all set to work clearing the table and doing the dishes, and everything was quickly cleaned up. Minutes later, Great Aunt Squeegee, Fribble, and Scamper headed down the street toward Pioneer Park. Great Aunt Squeegee carried an old towel. Scamper brought two scrubbing brushes, and Fribble had a plastic bucket half-full of hot, soapy water. He tried not to splash it too much as they walked along.

They went through the gate of the park, and Fribble led them to the rock beneath the tree. They set to work right away. Fribble and Scamper scrubbed and scrubbed. Then Great Aunt Squeegee vigorously polished until the brass marker was clean and shiny.

Now that he could read it, Fribble pulled out his notepad and carefully wrote down every word. "Ehrich Weiss, Handcuff King, Native Son of Wisconsin, a legend in his own time who performed in Cheddarville as a young man. Erected as a memorial on the first anniversary of his death, October 31, 1927, by his admiring pupil, TTM."

After the inscription, there was a line of music. Fribble copied this down, too, drawing five lines and being careful to place each note in the right place on the musical staff.

After he finished copying everything down, Fribble looked at Great Aunt Squeegee. "Have you ever heard of Ehrich Weiss?" he asked.

"No, I haven't," Great Aunt Squeegee admitted.

"And what's a Handcuff King?" asked Fribble.

"I didn't know Cheddarville ever had a king," Scamper said. "Did we have a queen, too? And a princess and a prince?" he added hopefully.

Fribble sighed. He knew that once Scamper got a wrong idea in his head, it would be hard to get it out again. "At least I know what handcuffs are," Fribble said. "They're the metal rings that policemen lock around the wrists of bad guys."

"Oh, yeah. I've seen those on TV," Scamper said. "Was Ehrich a bad guy?"

"I don't know," Fribble said. "Why would you put up a marker for a bad guy?"

"I think 'Handcuff King' must be a nickname," Great Aunt Squeegee said.

"Huh?" asked Scamper. "What's a nickname?"

Great Aunt Squeegee explained. "You know how everyone calls your uncle 'Dizzy.' That's because he always seems to be running around in circles. Dizzy is his nickname. So, whoever Ehrich Weiss is, he must have something to do with handcuffs."

"What a lot of mysteries," Fribble said. "Who's Ehrich Weiss? Why is he the Handcuff King? Who is TTM? And what did the Handcuff King teach him? And why is there music written here?"

"I don't know, Fribble," Great Aunt Squeegee said. "It makes me kind of dizzy just thinking about it. But I'll bet you'll figure it all out, and when you do, be sure to tell me."

They gathered up their cleaning tools and walked home. What a wonderful day, Fribble thought. He loved scuffling through the leaves, he loved being with Great Aunt Squeegee, and he loved having lots of mysteries to solve.

They got home and put their cleaning materials away. Great Aunt Squeegee finally agreed to sit down and rest for a few minutes.

"Could Scamper and I make another trip to the library?" Fribble asked.

"Of course," their mother agreed.

"We may stop at Tweek's house on our way home," Fribble added.

"All right," their mother said. "But don't be late for dinner."

Miss Scurry smiled when she saw them enter the library. "My best customers," she teased. "And what are the two of you looking for today?"

"We need to use an encyclopedia," Fribble said, and he led the way to where the set of encyclopedias was located. He knelt and looked at the words on each of their spines. He finally picked up volume 23, which was labeled "Vine to Zoology."

"The words starting with 'W' will be in this one," he explained to Scamper.

Fribble pulled out his notebook to check the spelling of the name he had written there. Then he began to look for Ehrich Weiss. "Here he is!" he shouted, smiling broadly and pointing to a picture of a man in a black suit with a bow tie. Then his smile vanished. "Oh, no," he said. "I'm wrong. This guy isn't named Weiss. He's named August Weismann."

Fribble looked for the entry before and after August Weismann. "I can't find Weiss," he said.

Miss Scurry, who had come over to help, leaned over Fribble and ran her paw down the page. "You're right," she said. "There is no Ehrich Weiss on this page."

Fribble's whiskers drooped. For the first time, the encyclopedia had failed him.

Fribble slammed the book shut. He frowned and said, "We'll never find out the rock's secrets. I guess Ehrich isn't famous enough to be in an encyclopedia."

"If he isn't famous, how come he got a marker?" asked Scamper.

"Now, wait," said Miss Scurry, jumping into their conversation. "Don't be so quick to give up on this book. Let's try the index."

"Index?" asked Fribble.

"Yes, the last book in a set of encyclopedias is an index to the whole set," Miss Scurry explained. "It's a listing of everything that's covered in the encyclopedia set, and it tells you where to look to find it."

"You mean he might still be in the encyclopedia even though he isn't listed under 'W' as Ehrich Weiss?"

"Could be." Miss Scurry went and got the book marked "Index" off the shelf and put it in front of Fribble. "It's alphabetical. See what you can find out."

Fribble took the index and flipped through pages until he reached the "W" listings. There were a lot of them. Slowly, he ran his paw down the small print until he got to Weiss. Then he looked for Ehrich. "It's here!" he shouted in a voice that could be heard all over the library. In his excitement, he'd forgotten all about using his indoor voice.

"What's it say?" Scamper crowded closer to his brother.

Fribble read and then he frowned. "I don't get it," he said in a softer voice. "It says, 'Weiss, Ehrich, see Houdini, Harry.'" Fribble stroked his whiskers thoughtfully. He looked at Miss Scurry. "If he's in the encyclopedia, why isn't he listed as Ehrich Weiss? And who's Houdini, Harry?"

Miss Scurry explained, "When he was born, he was named Ehrich Weiss. But he chose to use the name 'Harry Houdini.' And that's the name that became famous."

"Is Harry Houdini like a nickname?" asked Scamper, remembering what Great Aunt Squeegee had told them in the park.

Miss Scurry smiled at little Scamper. "Harry Houdini is something like a nickname, but usually we call it a 'stage name.' Lots of famous movie and television stars use stage names instead of their real names."

"Ooooh! Was Ehrich a movie star?" Scamper's eyes grew wide.

"Why don't you look up 'Harry Houdini' in the encyclopedia and find out," suggested Miss Scurry.

Fribble closed the index and went to look at the other volumes in the set. This time he chose Volume 11, which covered "Halifax to Illinois." "Harry Houdini should be in here somewhere," Fribble said, "under 'H'." He thumbed through the pages. And there, after a long article about horses, he finally found it. "Here it is," he squeaked, and he read aloud, "Houdini, Harry, 1874 to 1926."

"Wasn't our marker dated 1927?" asked Scamper. Fribble wondered once again how such a little guy could have such a long memory.

"You're right." Fribble looked at his notebook, which was still open on the table. "It is dated 1927.

But remember, the marker was put there one year after his death."

"Oh, yeah," Scamper said. "What else does it say?"

"It says Harry Houdini was a magician. He was known for his sensational escapes. He was born in Appleton, Wisconsin, and his real name was Ehrich Weiss. He became famous all over the world in the early 1900s. People came to see him escape from ropes and handcuffs and locked trunks."

"Wow!" said Scamper. "A magician who could escape from handcuffs."

"Yes," Fribble said. "This is definitely our guy. And it says he died in Detroit, Michigan, on Halloween in 1926."

"Mystery solved," said Miss Scurry with a smile.

"Well, one of our mysteries, anyway," Fribble said. "We have quite a lot of them. Gee, thanks, Miss Scurry. I didn't know that the encyclopedia had an index."

"Is there anything else I can help you with today?" Miss Scurry asked.

Fribble looked up at the big clock that hung on the library wall. "I don't think so," he said. "There's a lot more that I want to know, but it's almost five o'clock. We're going to stop at a friend's house, so we'd better get going or we'll be late for supper."

Fribble and Scamper left the library and made a slight detour from their regular route. It brought them straight to Tweek's house.

"Are we stopping at Tweek's to tell him what you learned about the marker on the rock?" asked Scamper.

"He'll be interested," Fribble said. "But my main reason for stopping is that Tweek has a piano. He takes lessons."

"Do you want Tweek to give you a piano lesson?" Scamper asked. "Will he give me a lesson, too?"

"No," Fribble said. "Don't you remember? There was a line of music written on the marker beneath the rock. Harry Houdini was a famous magician. So why would his marker have music on it?"

By this time they were on Tweek's doorstep, and Fribble rang the bell. Tweek let them in, and with only a few interruptions from Scamper, Fribble managed to tell Tweek what they had learned so far about the marker in the park. "I thought you could play this line of music, and maybe we could guess what it is."

Tweek took Fribble's little notebook over to the piano and propped it up on the music stand. Then he leaned in close so he could read it. Slowly he picked out the notes on the piano. Then Tweek played it a second time a little more quickly.

Just as he finished, Tweek's mother came into the room. "Why are you playing 'Auld Lang Syne'?" she asked with a smile.

"'Auld Lang Syne'? Is that the name of this song?" Fribble asked. "It sounds a little familiar."

"Yes," Tweek's mother said. "'Auld Lang Syne' means 'times long gone.' It's a very famous song that's usually played right at midnight on New Year's Eve."

"I thought I'd heard it before." Fribble glanced at the clock. "Thanks." He picked up his notebook and put it in his pocket. "We've got to hurry home. Our Great Aunt Squeegee is visiting, and we can't be late to supper."

As they walked the short distance home, Fribble hummed "Auld Lang Syne." He was puzzled as to why that music would be on Harry Houdini's marker.

When they came in their house, they found Great Aunt Squeegee sitting in the living room working a crossword puzzle. The table was all set

27

for dinner, and Fribble's mother was doing a few last-minute things in the kitchen.

Immediately, Great Aunt Squeegee stopped what she was doing and said, "Tell me everything you learned."

Fribble, with help from Scamper, told her.

"'Auld Lang Syne,'" Great Aunt Squeegee said. "What an unusual piece of music to have on a marker to a magician."

"Have you ever heard of Harry Houdini?" asked Fribble.

"Oh, yes," Great Aunt Squeegee said. "He was very famous."

"Monday, when I go to school, I'm going to see if there are any books about him in our library," Fribble said.

"You're making good progress in solving a conundrum," Great Aunt Squeegee said.

"What's a conundrum?" Fribble asked.

"A conundrum is a puzzle or a mystery," Great Aunt Squeegee explained. "As a matter of fact, it's a clue here in my crossword." She tapped her pencil on the puzzle in front of her. "The word I'm looking for means conundrum. But I can't figure it out.

It's got to be a word with six letters in it, and it's got to start with an 'R.'"

"Hmmm," Fribble looked at the space that Great Aunt Squeegee pointed to in the crossword. He stroked his whiskers and thought.

Scamper struck a pose just like his big brother and stroked his whiskers, too.

"Rrrrr," Fribble muttered to himself. "Rrrrr." What word could it be? Then suddenly he shouted, "Rrrrr-riddle? Could it be riddle?"

Great Aunt Squeegee smiled. "I think you've got it." Using her pencil, she wrote "riddle" into the six spaces. "Fribble, you're so good at puzzles."

Fribble beamed, and Scamper said, "I was just going to say 'riddle'."

"Fribble. Scamper. Time to wash your paws for dinner," their mother called. Something smelled delicious, and Fribble and Scamper ran to wash up.

As he scrubbed with soap, Fribble thought of all the conundrums he still had to solve from the marker beneath the rock. When had Houdini been in Cheddarville? Who was his pupil? Why was "Auld Lang Syne" on the marker? But at least now he knew that Ehrich Weiss was Harry Houdini, the famous magician. That's where he'd start in the library at school on Monday morning.

Monday morning when they reached school, Fribble left Scamper by the swings on the first grade playground. Then, he hurried to the library. Miss Longwhiskers always let students come into the library before classes started to return and check out books.

"Good morning," Miss Longwhiskers said to Fribble when he came in. "Just returning books, or do you need any help today?"

"I'm looking for a biography," Fribble said.

"Aha," said Miss Longwhiskers. "And whose biography are you looking for?"

"Harry Houdini," said Fribble.

"Really? I didn't know you were interested in magic and magicians, Fribble."

"Oh, yes," Fribble said. "When my class went to Pioneer Park to do a clean up, I found an old marker that's a memorial to Harry Houdini."

"How interesting. Do you know how to spell that name so that you can look it up in the computer card catalog?" Miss Longwhiskers asked.

Fribble pulled his little spiral notebook from his back pocket. "I have it written down right here."

Fribble went over to the computer and typed in "Harry Houdini." Two titles came up.

Miss Longwhiskers looked at the screen. "Do you remember how to tell which books are biographies for young readers?" she asked.

Fribble thought for a minute. "Yes," he said. With his paw, he pointed to the first title. "This one called *Harry Houdini, Escape Artist* has JB Houdini after it. The 'J' is for juvenile, or kids, and the 'B Houdini' means it's a biography of Harry Houdini."

"Good for you, Fribble," Miss Longwhiskers said. "And what about this one?" She asked, pointing to the second title on the screen.

Fribble read it carefully. *Harry Houdini, Young Magician.* It was also followed by JB Houdini. "Yes!" Fribble was excited. "There are two biographies about Harry Houdini." Then he said, "But look. Instead of saying 'checked out' or 'shelf,' this one says 'lost.'"

"You're right," Miss Longwhiskers said. "Sorry about that. I've noticed that books about magicians and magic often have a way of disappearing."

"Really?" asked Fribble, as he looked at Miss Longwhiskers. She had a twinkle in her eye. He thought maybe she was joking. He wasn't sure what he would do if the book he was reading about Harry Houdini disappeared into thin air.

Miss Longwhiskers smiled. "They don't go 'poof' and disappear," she said. "But they are very popular books. Students sometimes take them home and keep them for a long time. They seem to 'disappear' into closets and backpacks, and beneath beds. Lots of them reappear at the end of the school year when we have our Lost Book Round Up. But until it's found, we only have one biography on Houdini."

Miss Longwhiskers led Fribble over to a section marked Biographies. "We keep all the biographies in a special place in our library." She pointed to a

shelf of books. "Here they are, alphabetical by the famous person's name. So you'll look in the 'H' section for Houdini."

Fribble quickly found the Houdini biography and held it tightly in his paws.

"I wish someone hadn't lost that other book," he said. "I want to read all I can about Harry Houdini and his magic tricks."

"We don't have another biography on Houdini, but there are books in the nonfiction section about magicians and magic tricks," Miss Longwhiskers said. "Check the card catalog again."

Fribble entered "magic tricks," into the computer catalog and several new titles came up. They all had the call number 793.8. Fribble scurried off into the stacks again. In his school, you were only allowed to check out three books at a time, so Fribble looked at several books on magic tricks before he finally picked the two he wanted to check out. The ones he chose had lots of pictures showing exactly how to do the tricks.

He left the library with his three books tucked under his arm just as the first bell rang. Fribble hurried to line up at the door with his class.

His best friend, Tweek, was in line waiting for him. Tweek dropped back to stand with Fribble, and Fribble showed him the books he had checked out. "I'm going to read all three of these tonight," he said.

When Fribble arrived home after school, that's exactly what he did. First, he had a snack of cheese and crackers with Great Aunt Squeegee and Scamper. Then he went to his room and did his homework. Finally he started to read his library books.

Fribble hadn't read much before Scamper slipped into his room to ask, "Will you read to me about Harry Houdini?"

"Sure," Fribble said, and he began to read aloud. He stopped and read the same sentence twice. "This can't be," Fribble said.

"What can't be?" asked Scamper.

"It says right here, 'Houdini's real name was Ehrich Weiss.'"

"We already knew that," Scamper pointed out.

"But listen," Fribble said. "Then it says, 'and he was born in Budapest, Hungary.'"

Fribble sounded out these last two words as best he could.

"Where's that?" asked Scamper.

"I don't know exactly," Fribble said. He stroked his long whiskers. "But it's definitely not Appleton, Wisconsin." He pulled out his notebook and opened it to the page where he had copied down what was written on the marker.

"The marker says that Ehrich Weiss was a native son of Wisconsin," Fribble told his little brother. "I thought that being a native son meant he was born in Wisconsin."

"Let's ask Great Aunt Squeegee," said Scamper.

Taking the book with them, they hurried downstairs to the living room. Fribble showed her his notebook. "What does being a native son of Wisconsin mean?" he asked.

"It means being born in Wisconsin," Great Aunt Squeegee said.

"That's what I thought. But look in this book." Fribble leaned over the arm of the big, stuffed chair and laid the open book on Great Aunt Squeegee's lap. He pointed with his paw. "It says right here that Harry Houdini was born in," Fribble hesitated, and then he again sounded out the two words as best he could, "Budapest, Hungary."

"Budapest, Hungary, is clear across the Atlantic Ocean in Europe," Great Aunt Squeegee said. "How strange. If Harry Houdini was born in Hungary, he wasn't a native son of Wisconsin." She shook her head. "I guess you have another mystery on your hands, Fribble."

"I wonder if this is a mistake," Fribble said. "Our school has another biography of Harry Houdini, but that book is lost. It might tell me if Houdini was born in Wisconsin or if he was born in Hungary."

"Maybe the public library has another biography of Houdini," Great Aunt Squeegee suggested. "Then you could compare the two."

Fribble glanced at the mantle clock. There was just enough time to visit the library and still get home for dinner.

Fribble ran to the kitchen to tell his mother where he was going.

"Can I come, too?" Scamper asked.

"Sure," Fribble agreed.

As they walked, Fribble said, "Remember Harry Houdini was listed in the encyclopedia, too. I'll bet it tells where he was born. That's another place to look."

As soon as they reached the library, Fribble went straight to the encyclopedia. This time he looked up Ehrich Weiss under the name of Harry Houdini.

"What's it say?" asked Scamper.

"It says Harry Houdini was born in Appleton, Wisconsin."

"Then he's a native son," said Scamper. His whiskers quivered.

"I wonder which is right," Fribble said. He led the way to the computer catalog and typed in Harry Houdini. Up came a title that Fribble hadn't seen at school, *Escape King: The Story of Harry Houdini.* Fribble copied down the number, 793.8092. He hurried to the shelves, and Scamper trailed right along with him.

They found three books, side by side, about Harry Houdini. Fribble carried all of them over to a table and began to read. "This one says that Harry Houdini was born in Budapest, Hungary, and was brought to Appleton, Wisconsin, when he was a little boy."

He closed that book and opened another. "This one says his father came to Appleton, Wisconsin, and his wife and sons came later when Harry was four years old."

"What does this book say?" asked Scamper, as he handed him the third book.

Fribble read and then he said, "I guess this sort of explains it. It says, 'Harry Houdini wanted to please American audiences, so he often said he was born in Appleton, Wisconsin, but he was really born in Budapest, Hungary.'"

"So he isn't a native son of Wisconsin," said Scamper.

"No," Fribble said. "I guess the encyclopedia is wrong this time. The great magician played a trick on them." He grinned at Scamper.

Fribble studied the Harry Houdini biographies. He learned a lot about the Handcuff King, but he still had plenty of questions. When had the great magician come to Cheddarville? Fribble squeezed his eyes tight and tried to imagine it. Oh, how he wished he'd been able to see him perform. Who was his lucky pupil? Why was "Auld Lang Syne" on the marker? None of this was mentioned in any of the books.

Hoping to amaze people as the great Houdini had, Fribble began to study magic tricks. From the books he'd read, he learned that you didn't just jump up and do tricks. It was important to set the stage for your audience. You had to dress up, practice, learn to talk fast and make people look where you wanted them to. In the meantime, you did fancy tricks with your hands. Tricks that you had practiced over and over.

Fribble scurried through the house gathering up what he needed. He got cards, coins, a scarf, a handkerchief, string, rope, an egg, balloons, a hat, and paper bags. Then he went back to his room, shut the door, and practiced. As he tried the tricks, he studied the pictures in his books and talked out loud.

Scamper came to see what Fribble was doing. "Why are you talking to yourself?" Scamper asked.

"I'm working on my magic show. It's almost ready. Sit down. You can be my audience." Fribble wished he had a tall silk hat. But he didn't, so he put on his best jacket and a felt hat of his father's. The hat was a little too big, and Fribble had to keep pushing it up, or he couldn't see.

Scamper took a seat on the antique chest at the foot of the bed. Fribble picked up an old jump rope. "Ladies and gentlemen," Fribble announced, "Watch while I tie the fastest knot in the world. My paws move so quickly, you will only see a blur." Fribble held up the rope with his paws far apart. Then he brought his paws together and quickly pulled them apart again. "Shazaam! Behold the knot," he cried, as he held up the rope in front of Scamper's eyes. But there was no knot in the rope.

"Drat! I guess I did something wrong," Fribble said. "I'll have to study that trick some more. But on with the show!" He tossed the rope on the bed and pushed up his hat again so he could see. "Now for a famous coin trick. Watch carefully." Fribble put a coin in each of his paws and held them open in front of Scamper. "I shall make this coin disappear." Fribble quickly turned over his paws. "Shazaam!" he cried as he opened an empty paw.

"Hey!" Scamper said. "I saw you toss a coin from one paw to the other."

"Well, you weren't supposed to see that," Fribble said. He frowned. "I'll try again." Fribble held both coins out in his open paws, and then he quickly flipped his paws over again. This time one of the coins fell on the floor and his hat fell off, too.

Fribble sighed as he picked up the hat and jammed it back on his head. "I guess I need more practice on that trick, too. But hey, I've got a good trick with a hanky, a hat, and an egg. Want to see?"

Scamper looked at the coin that had fallen on the floor. Then he looked at his father's hat. "Maybe

you should practice a little more before you do a trick with eggs," he suggested.

"How about a card trick then? Would you like to see my card trick, Scamper?"

"Sure," Scamper said.

Fribble brought out a deck of cards and held half in each paw. "Pick a card from one paw, look at it, remember what it is, and put it with the cards in the other paw. And don't let me see it."

Scamper followed directions. Fribble put both piles of cards together. Then, slowly, one by one, he looked through them. "Think hard about your card," he ordered. "I'll read your mind and find it." After looking at several cards, and pretending to concentrate, Fribble finally pulled out the four of diamonds. "Shazaam! This is the card you picked."

"Hey! You're right." Scamper sounded surprised. "How did you do that?"

"Like the famous magician Harry Houdini always said, 'Never explain a magic trick.'" Fribble bowed and his hat fell off again. "That concludes my show. But after I learn more tricks, you can be my audience again."

Tuesday, at school during library period, Fribble returned the two magic books he'd read and checked out new ones. He planned to study these when he got home and practice his tricks over and over.

Then Fribble hurried to a library computer that was connected to the Internet. He typed in "Harry Houdini," and lots of items came up on the screen.

Fribble's nose began to twitch with excitement when he saw that one of the articles was written by Harry Houdini himself! "Wow!" Fribble whispered. He began to read the article called "Harry Houdini" by Harry Houdini. It was dated London, 1910. The very first sentence said, "My birth occurred April 6th, 1874, in the small town of Appleton, in the State of Wisconsin."

Fribble shook his head in disbelief. No wonder people who wrote books about this famous magician were confused. Harry Houdini didn't always write the truth.

Fribble read through several of the articles on the Internet. He was running out of time just as he found an entry called "Harry Houdini Biography." It was six pages long.

Fribble scurried over to Miss Longwhiskers. "I've found a good article on Harry Houdini, but I don't have time to read it."

"We can print it out, and you can take it home to study," she said. She showed Fribble how to print it from the computer screen.

Fribble read the article that night after he finished his homework. The article quoted a pamphlet written by Harry Houdini in which he said that his favorite song was the traditional New Year's Eve tune, "Auld Lang Syne," and that he often had this song played at the end of his magic shows.

"Aha!" Fribble shouted right out loud. "So that's why that line of music was on the marker in Pioneer Park." He ran to tell Scamper, Great Aunt Squeegee, and his mother what he had discovered.

"So," said Great Aunt Squeegee, stopping work on her crossword puzzle to listen to the latest news from Fribble, "have you discovered all of the secrets beneath the rock?"

"Not all of them," Fribble admitted. "I know now that Ehrich Weiss was the real name of Harry Houdini. He was a famous magician known as the Handcuff King, and 'Auld Lang Syne' was his favorite song. And I know that he wasn't really a native son of Wisconsin, even though he told everyone that he was. But I don't know when he came to Cheddarville or who his pupil, TTM, was."

"Well, you're such a good detective, I'm sure you'll find out," Great Aunt Squeegee said. "In the meantime, maybe you can help me with my puzzle. I'm stuck again."

"Sure." Fribble puffed out his chest. "I'll try. What are the clues?"

"I need a four letter word ending in 'e.' The clue is 'epistle.'"

Fribble's whiskers drooped, and his chest unpuffed. "I'm sorry, but I don't know what epistle means."

"An epistle is a sort of fancy message or letter," Great Aunt Squeegee explained. "But 'message' and 'letter' are too long to fit in the puzzle space." She furrowed her brow.

"Hmmm." Fribble stood very still and stroked his whiskers. Scamper, who had been watching a TV program, turned his back on the set, looked thoughtful and stroked his whiskers, too.

"Epistle, message, letter. Hmmm. How about ... 'note'?" said Fribble.

"Good idea," said Great Aunt Squeegee, and she penciled the word in the puzzle. "You're a big help, Fribble." She smiled at him.

"And that reminds me," said Fribble. "My teacher sent home a fancy note today all decorated in autumn leaves about the Fall Festival. I'll get it. It's in my backpack."

Fribble ran up to his room and when he came back down, he brought the note from school with him. He smoothed it out and said, "I'll read it to you."

Fribble read aloud, "The Fall Festival will be Friday night, November 17, at four o'clock in the afternoon. There'll be games, food, a cakewalk, and a show on stage in the gym at eight o'clock. You may buy tickets for different activities for a quarter at the door. Invite all your friends and neighbors. Any profits go for playground equipment and library books."

Fribble handed the note to his mother who put on her reading glasses.

"Maybe we could invite our friends, Miss Slippers from the antique shop and Mr. Crumb from across the street," Scamper suggested.

"Good idea," his mother said. "And there's a place here to sign up for anything we can do to help. You can bring cheese and crackers to the food table, donate a cake for the cakewalk, set up a booth, or volunteer to do an act on stage. The note needs to be filled out, signed, and sent back by this Friday."

"My goodness," Great Aunt Squeegee said. "What an exciting night! I'm so glad I'm going to be here. You may certainly sign me up to bring a cake for the cakewalk."

"Goody!" squeaked Scamper. "I'm going to try to win it!"

"And I'm going to sign up to be in the show," Fribble said.

His mother looked surprised. "You are?"

"Yes, I'm going to perform magic tricks."

"Are you sure you can be ready?" Scamper asked. He looked worried.

"Of course!" Fribble said. "The Fall Festival is a whole week off. I just need a little more practice." And with that, he went back upstairs to study his magic tricks again.

On Wednesday morning, once the third grade class had finally quieted down, Mrs. Tremble asked her class to turn in their Fall Festival notes. Wild excitement broke out again as students scrambled to retrieve them from backpacks and notebooks.

"I'm glad that so many of you remembered to bring these back to school today," Mrs. Tremble said, holding up a pawful of notes. "And if you forgot, that's all right. I'll be collecting notes again tomorrow and Friday. I hope that you and your family and friends will all be able to come. I think our Fall Festival is going to be a very special evening."

Fribble closed his eyes tightly for a moment and imagined how it would feel next week to stand on stage in the school auditorium. He'd amaze everyone with his fantastic magic tricks. He could almost hear the thundering applause as he finished. Then, his eyes snapped open. An idea had popped into his head. A great idea! It was hard to wait for recess so that he could share it with Tweek.

When the recess bell finally rang, and the third and fourth graders poured out the door and onto the playground, Fribble went straight to Tweek. "Guess what?"

"What?" Tweek asked.

"I'm going to perform in the show at the Fall Festival," Fribble said.

"You are?"

"Yes, and I want you to perform, too."

"Me?" Tweek let out a little squeak of surprise.

"Yes, I want you to be my assistant."

"What does your assistant do?" asked Tweek.

"For one thing," Fribble said, "I want you to play the piano. I want you to play 'Auld Lang Syne.'"

"Why would I play 'Auld Lang Syne' in November? That's a New Year's Eve song."

"Because I'm doing a magic show," Fribble explained, "just like Harry Houdini. And Houdini always had that song played at the end of his show."

"A magic show?" Tweek said. "When did you learn magic?"

"I just started a few days ago," Fribble confessed. "But I've got some good books and they show exactly how to do the tricks. But sometimes I need an assistant. That's where you come in."

"Gee, I don't know," Tweek said. "I guess my music teacher and my mom could help me learn how to play 'Auld Lang Syne' by next week, at least with one paw. But I don't know how to do any magic tricks."

"We'll practice," Fribble said. "You could come over right after school today and we'll start."

"I can't," Tweek said. "I have piano lessons on Wednesdays."

"Oh, that's all right," Fribble said. "We have plenty of time to practice our magic tricks. And that means you can start to learn 'Auld Lang Syne' this afternoon."

Pleased that Tweek would soon be learning to play Houdini's favorite song, Fribble daydreamed all day about how great his magic show would be.

After school, Fribble thought he should practice his magic tricks even if Tweek couldn't. He went to his room and tried tying the knot in the rope again. But no matter how hard he tried, or how carefully he studied the diagram in the book, no knot ever appeared in the rope. What if he couldn't learn his tricks in time for the show? Fribble felt a moment of panic. He tossed the rope aside and plopped down on the bed.

Had Houdini practiced this hard? Had he ever failed? Or had it been easy for him? Fribble found himself thinking about the young magician who wanted so much to please his audience in his new country that he even pretended to be a native son of Wisconsin.

"Whatcha doing?" Scamper asked, as he came bouncing into Fribble's room.

"Thinking."

"About what?"

"I've been thinking about Harry Houdini and how it must have been hard for him to come to America when he was only four years old."

"Yeah," Scamper agreed. "He must have missed all his friends back home. Hey, I forget. What's the name of that country he was from?"

"He was from Budapest, Hungary," Fribble reminded him.

"Kind of a funny name, isn't it? Do you know where that is?"

"No," Fribble admitted. And since he was tired of practicing magic tricks that didn't work, he said, "Want to go to the library and find out?"

"Sure," Scamper said.

A few minutes later, they were bounding up the steps of the library to Miss Scurry's desk. "How can I help you today?" she asked with a smile.

"We need to use the atlas," Fribble explained.

"What are you looking for this time?" Miss Scurry asked.

"Budapest, Hungary."

Miss Scurry went to get the big atlas from the reference shelf. She carried it to a table. "Do you remember how to use this?"

"Yes," Fribble said. "I'll look in the index."

"All right. Now I'm going to help that woman standing by my desk. But I'll come back if you need me."

Fribble turned to the index at the back of the big book of maps and ran his paw down the H's until he

found the name Hungary. "It says Hungary is located on page 49, at H and 7," he told Scamper.

"I can find page 49," Scamper said, and he did, although it took him a while.

"Now, we're looking for 7 and H. It's a kind of a grid," Fribble explained. He ran one paw across from the 7 that was in the left margin of the page, and one paw up from the letter H at the bottom of the page until his paws met. "Here it is! Hungary. And here's Budapest, too."

"Is that a long way from Wisconsin?" Scamper asked.

"Yeah. It's a real long way. Let me show you." Fribble opened the atlas to a map of the world and he showed Scamper where Wisconsin was. Then he moved his paw to New York, and then all the way across the Atlantic Ocean to Hungary.

While they were studying the map, Miss Scurry came back. "Now you've got me curious," she said. "Why are you looking up Budapest, Hungary?"

"At first we thought that Ehrich Weiss, or Harry Houdini, was born in Appleton, Wisconsin," Fribble said. "But he wasn't. He just told people that story because he wanted them to think he was an American. He was really born in Budapest, Hungary.

The entry in the encyclopedia about where he was born is wrong," he explained.

"That's very interesting," Miss Scurry said. "You two are becoming real library detectives."

Fribble and Scamper smiled.

"You know, I was hoping that I'd see you soon," Miss Scurry went on. "Because I have been saving something interesting to show you. It may be another clue."

"A clue?" Fribble said. His tail began lashing back and forth and his whiskers quivered. "What sort of a clue?"

Miss Scurry returned to her desk. It was all Fribble could do not to run after her. He didn't want to wait even an extra second for the clue she had promised to share with him. What could it be? His nose twitched as he forced himself to sit still.

As Fribble watched, Miss Scurry took something from beneath her desk. When she headed back, she carried a sheet of paper.

"The last time you were in here, you talked about the rock in the park, and you said that Houdini had died on Halloween. After you left, I got to thinking about that. And I recalled reading a special article in the newspaper just last month on the history of Halloween in Cheddarville. I couldn't remember the details, but I was pretty sure it mentioned Houdini. I thought maybe you'd like to read it. So I looked up the article in our newspaper file, and I photocopied it for you." She handed it to Fribble.

"Gee, thanks," Fribble cried. He put the copy on the table and began to read it while Miss Scurry went to help someone else.

"What's it say?" asked Scamper.

"The article is called 'A History of Halloween in Cheddarville: Tricks, Treats, Spooks, and Magic,'" said Fribble. "And it tells things that happened in our town on Halloween over the past 100 years. There are pictures, too. Look. Here's one of a big fire that happened on Halloween 20 years ago. It burned up a restaurant."

"Wow!" Scamper said, as he studied the old newspaper photo.

"And here's a picture of Main Street covered in snow. 'An early blizzard hit Cheddarville on Halloween back in 1920.'" Fribble read the caption and pointed to a snow scene.

"Does it say anything about Houdini?" asked Scamper.

"It must," Fribble said. "But I don't see it. I guess I'd better read this from beginning to end." So Fribble started at the beginning and slowly read the article, word by word.

The reporter who had written the story had interviewed lots of different people, especially old-timers who remembered Halloweens in Cheddarville from long ago. "Here's something!" Fribble suddenly said. "Listen to this."

Fribble read aloud to Scamper, "Perhaps the most amazing magic to ever be seen in Cheddarville happened more than 100 years ago. In 1901, the famous magician, Harry Houdini, performed in Cheddarville. This reporter interviewed a citizen of Cheddarville who showed him an old poster, handed down through his family, advertising the event. He told this reporter that his great-great-great-great-great-grandfather had persuaded Houdini to put on a magic show. The poster said the highlight of that show would be the Vanishing Birdcage." Fribble stopped reading. He sat there for a moment, thinking.

"What else does it say?" asked Scamper.

"That's all it says about Houdini," Fribble said. "It doesn't give the name of the person who the reporter interviewed. And he doesn't say who his great-great-great-great-great-grandfather was."

"So, I guess it doesn't help us, huh?" said Scamper.

"Oh, it helps a lot," Fribble said. "Miss Scurry is right. This is a valuable clue. We know now that Houdini performed in Cheddarville in 1901. And the reporter who wrote this story last month probably knows a lot more about it."

"Who is he?" asked Scamper.

"Let's see." Fribble looked at the beginning of the article again. "His name is Scribble McCarthy."

"How can we find him?" Scamper asked.

"Call the newspaper, I guess. But it's almost dinnertime. We'll have to wait till tomorrow to do that."

Before they left the library, Fribble thanked Miss Scurry again for sharing the newspaper article with him. "I'll be following up on this, and I'll let you know what I learn," he promised. Fribble felt good knowing that he had a real clue to chase down.

Scamper and Fribble hurried home to dinner. Great Aunt Squeegee was taking a turn at cooking dinner tonight. "I'm fixing something easy. Your favorite, Fribble, macaroni and cheese."

Fribble gave Great Aunt Squeegee a hug.

"Anything we can do to help?" Fribble asked, sniffing the air in delight.

"Yes, you two are just in time to set the table."

Scamper carefully counted out the forks and spoons, as Fribble folded the napkins and put them at each place. Seeing the napkins reminded Fribble of something. "I've been practicing a magic trick that you do with a napkin or a scarf," he said. "Want to see?"

"Of course," Great Aunt Squeegee said. "We can have a short show before dinner while we're waiting for the cheese to get bubbly in the oven."

"I'll just be a minute," Fribble said. He scurried off upstairs.

Fribble had been practicing this trick for two days, and he was sure that he could do it. He had taken a thin piece of elastic that his mother had given him from her sewing box. He had cut the end out of a dented table ping-pong ball. And then he had taped the ball to the elastic.

Now with a safety pin, Fribble pinned the other end of the elastic to his shirt pocket. Fribble put on his father's hat and his suit jacket. Then he pulled the elastic across his chest. He buttoned the bottom button. Fribble was careful to leave the elastic with the ball attached sticking out the front of his jacket just above the button. Then Fribble reached up and hid the ball in his left paw with the elastic pulled tight. In his right paw, he picked up a red, silk scarf. Ready at last, Fribble raced down the stairs.

Great Aunt Squeegee and Scamper had joined Mom in the living room. They all sat on the couch, and Fribble faced them. "Ladies and gentlemen," Fribble announced. "You are about to see an astonishing piece of magic." He waved the bright red silk scarf in front of them. "I shall make this scarf vanish right before your eyes."

Fribble began to stuff the silk scarf into his left paw. As he stuffed, he made sure that it went inside the hollow ball that he held. Then he waved his right paw high in the air, and shouted "Shazaam!" At the same moment, he released the ball, now stuffed with the silk scarf, which shot out of sight underneath his suit jacket. Fribble opened both paws to show that they were empty. "Ta-da!"

Great Aunt Squeegee led the applause. Scamper whistled and cheered. "You did it," he shouted. "You really made it disappear!"

Fribble, feeling flushed with success, took a deep bow, and his hat fell off.

After the applause stopped, his mother said, "All right, Fribble and Scamper. Time to wash up for dinner."

Fribble scurried back upstairs to put his magic things away and to wash his paws. As the two of them came rushing back down the stairs, Scamper looked at his brother and said, "You really did it, Fribble. I didn't think you could, but you made the silk scarf disappear!"

"Yeah," Fribble said. "But I wonder how Houdini made a birdcage disappear?"

"I don't know," Scamper said, looking up at his brother with admiration. "But you've still got lots of time to figure it out!"

"Tomorrow after school," Fribble said, "I'm going to call the newspaper and find out what Scribble McCarthy can tell us about Houdini."

Thursday morning, while standing in line outside their classroom door, Fribble asked Tweek, "How is 'Auld Lang Syne' coming along?"

Tweek smiled. "When my piano teacher heard I'd be playing it on stage at school, he got pretty excited. We spent almost my whole lesson working on it. He says if I practice hard every day, I'll be able to do it."

"Good for you!" Fribble said. "And can you come over after school today to practice magic tricks?"

"Yeah, I already asked my mom."

After school, Fribble, Tweek, and Scamper hurried home. Great Aunt Squeegee had a snack of warm cheese puffs ready for them in the kitchen. "You're going to practice magic tricks?" she asked.

"Yes, right after I make a phone call," Fribble said.

"Who do you have to call?" Tweek asked.

"A reporter at the *Cheddarville Times.*" As Fribble dialed the number printed in the newspaper, he said, "Last month, Scribble McCarthy wrote a Halloween article in the newspaper that told about the magic show Harry Houdini gave in Cheddarville more than a hundred years ago."

When Scribble McCarthy answered, Fribble told the reporter about finding the marker on the stone in the park and getting interested in Harry Houdini. "I've solved most of the mysteries hidden under that old rock in Pioneer Park. But I sure would like to know more about Houdini's visit to Cheddarville and his pupil."

"I know someone who may be able to help you," Scribble McCarthy said. "Just a minute while I check my notes." There was a pause. "Ah, yes. Here it is. I went to the local magic shop and talked with the owner there. He's the one who had the old poster from 1901. The name of the shop is Abracadabra Magic Shop. It's at 99 Main Street."

"Thanks!" After he hung up the phone, Fribble told the others what he had learned. He stroked his whiskers. Fribble knew he should go straight upstairs and practice magic tricks with Tweek. But he was awfully anxious to visit the Abracadabra Magic Shop, too.

Great Aunt Squeegee seemed to know that he was being pulled in two directions. "If you'd like," she said, "I could drive you to the magic shop tomorrow after school and you could talk with the owner then. But perhaps you should call him first and see if that would be convenient."

Fribble grabbed the phone book and turned to the yellow pages where businesses were listed. To his surprise, there were four listings under "magicians." Three were for magicians who came to entertain at birthday parties, and one was for the Abracadabra Magic Shop.

Quickly Fribble dialed the number while Scamper and Tweek leaned close to listen in. When someone answered the phone, Fribble introduced himself and explained that he had read the newspaper article about Cheddarville's past Halloween celebrations and was very interested in Harry Houdini. "Scribble McCarthy from the *Cheddarville Times* told me about you. Could I come talk with you at 3:30 tomorrow?"

The shop owner said that would be fine. Thrilled, Fribble thanked him and hung up.

Fribble was beaming when he said, "He'll see us tomorrow!"

"What's his name?" Tweek asked.

Fribble looked shocked. "I don't know. I forgot to ask." He struck his forehead with his paw. "How could I be so stupid?"

"It doesn't matter," Great Aunt Squeegee said. "We'll drive down tomorrow right after school, and you'll meet him."

Fribble relaxed again. "Okay, Tweek, let's go to my room and make magic."

"Can I come, too?" asked Scamper.

Fribble looked at his eager little brother. He hated to disappoint him, but he and Tweek really did have to concentrate, and Fribble wanted to keep his magic tricks secret. Again Great Aunt Squeegee came to the rescue.

"Why don't we let them practice until they're ready for an audience?" she suggested to Scamper. "And in the meantime, you and I can have a tea party."

Scamper, who first looked as if he were going to object loudly to being shut out, dissolved into smiles. He scurried to get the sugar bowl and put it on the table.

Up in his room, Fribble put on his jacket and his father's hat and showed Tweek his magic show supplies. "I figure in five minutes, I can do three tricks," he said. "I can do the first and third trick by myself, but I need your help with the second one. First let me show you the Vanishing Scarf." Fribble showed his trick to Tweek. "Ta-da!"

"Hey, that's good. What's the second trick?" Tweek asked.

"I've been studying this balloon trick," Fribble said. He picked up a blue balloon. "See, I've stuffed a yellow balloon inside the blue one." He held it up and showed Tweek. "Your job is to pick up the balloons, being sure you hold on to the mouths of both of them, and blow them up as if they're one balloon. Try it."

Tweek picked up the balloon that had a second balloon tucked inside. He held both the mouths and blew them up. His little cheeks bulged, and he was soon out of breath. When he finished blowing, he held on tightly to the balloon mouths so that the air would not leak out.

"Good," Fribble said. "It looks like just one balloon. Now this is the tricky part, I'll stand next to you and say, 'Tweek, I think your balloon needs a little more air.' You keep the inner balloon pinched

tight while you blow a little more air into the outer balloon. Okay?"

Tweek gave another puff, and the balloons got away. They slipped out of his hand and shot around the room. Quickly, Tweek picked them up and blew up both balloons again. Then, although it wasn't easy, he used both paws and managed to follow Fribble's directions to add a little more air to the outer balloon.

"Now," Fribble said. "I'll say, 'ladies and gentlemen, watch closely while I magically change the color of this balloon.'" Fribble had quietly taken a pin from the sleeve of his jacket while Tweek was blowing more air into the balloon. Then he waved his hand with the pin in it over the balloon. As he said "Shazaam!" he pricked the outer blue balloon. It popped, suddenly revealing the yellow one inside.

Tweek gave a little gasp of surprise when the outer blue balloon went BANG!, but he held on tightly.

"Perfect! We take a bow." Fribble gave a deep bow and, as usual, his father's hat fell off. He picked it up. "Then you go over to the piano, and get ready to play as soon as I finish the last trick."

"What are you going to do for your last trick?"

"I'm not sure." Fribble sighed. "I've tried to tie a quick knot in a rope, and I've tried making a coin disappear, but so far I can't do either one right. I can do a mind-reading trick with cards. For it, I'd have to ask someone in the audience to volunteer to pick a card, and then I could tell them what it was."

"Sounds great!" Tweek said. "It gets the audience involved."

"Okay, and as my volunteer goes back to his seat, you can start 'Auld Lang Syne.' I'll walk over to the piano, and we'll both take a final bow."

"Wow! It's going to be a really neat act."

"It would be even better with Houdini's 1901 Halloween trick," Fribble said. "He did the Vanishing Birdcage. Oh, well. There was only one Harry Houdini."

"Wait till people see Fribble the Fabulous Magician. They'll love you," Tweek insisted.

"Let's go downstairs and present our whole act to Scamper, Mom, and Great Aunt Squeegee and see what they think."

The next day Fribble, Scamper, and Tweek rushed home after school to Fribble's house. His mother had a snack waiting for them on the table. They gobbled up the sesame seed crackers without their usual chatter. When Great Aunt Squeegee walked into the kitchen carrying her purse and wearing a hat, all three of them were ready to run right out and climb into her car.

Scamper sat up front with Great Aunt Squeegee, while Fribble and Tweek sat together in the back seat. They parked on Main Street and hurried toward the middle of the block. When they came to the front of the Abracadabra Magic Shop, all four paused to look in the window.

"Oooh! Look at that magic wand," Scamper said.

"And that black top hat," said Fribble.

"I love those bright silk scarves," Great Aunt Squeegee said.

"I like that fancy deck of cards," Tweek added.

But they didn't stand around long admiring the window display. Fribble was anxious to meet the owner, and he hustled everyone through the door.

The moment they stepped inside, a tall, slender mouse who had been standing behind the counter hurried forward and asked, "May I help you?"

"I hope so," Fribble said. He'd been expecting an older mouse, and this clerk was young. "My name is Fribble Mouse. I phoned you yesterday afternoon."

"Ah, yes," said the tall, elegant mouse. "I'm so pleased to meet you. Let me introduce myself. My name is Tip-Toe Macey Jr." He held out his paw.

As Fribble reached out and gripped the store owner's paw, his mind raced in high gear. Tip-Toe Macey. TTM. Hmmm. Those were the initials on the marker in the park. But how could that be? This was a young mouse, and that marker was very old.

Fribble's heart was beating so fast and so loudly that he was afraid the others would surely hear it.

"I'm Fribble's Great Aunt Squeegee, and this is Scamper and Tweek," Great Aunt Squeegee said, stepping forward and completing the introductions.

"How did you become interested in the Great Houdini?" asked Tip-Toe.

In a great rush, Fribble told him all about the rock in Pioneer Park and his efforts since then to uncover the secrets of the marker.

"I'm so sorry to hear that the granite stone rolled off its base," Tip-Toe said. "I will arrange to have it put back in place right away. I must say that you have been a very good detective in tracking down so many clues." Tip-Toe smiled at Fribble.

"But there's one thing I still don't know," Fribble said. "Who was the Great Houdini's pupil, the one who put up the marker to him in the park?"

"That would be my great-great-great-great-great-grandfather, Tip-Toe Macey Sr. He lived right here in Cheddarville and was the first magician in our family. You know that Houdini grew up in Appleton, not far from here. The original Tip-Toe Macey went to see a magic show there when he was a young mouse. He was so thrilled by the Great Houdini that he signed on for the summer to be his pupil and assistant."

"So that's how they met," Fribble said.

"Yes," said Tip-Toe. "And the following year, when Houdini came back from St. Louis to visit his family, he stopped in Cheddarville to see his old pupil. That's when Houdini agreed to put on a show for Tip-Toe."

"Wow!" Fribble said. "And that was more than 100 years ago."

"And my great-great-great-great-great-grandfather used his profits from that show to buy his first magic shop."

"Was this the shop?" asked Fribble glancing to the right and left and trying to take everything in at once.

"Oh, no. That first shop was in an old section of town that has since been torn down. But someone in our family has run a magic shop in Cheddarville ever since. My grandfather opened this shop. My father ran it. And now it's my turn."

"Are you a magician, too?" asked Scamper.

Tip-Toe stood very tall, twirled his whiskers, and said, "Why, of course."

"Do you know how to do the Vanishing Birdcage trick?" asked Fribble.

"How did you hear about that trick?" asked Tip-Toe. "It's very special."

"Scribble McCarthy wrote about the old poster you showed him. It advertised that the Great Houdini would perform the Vanishing Birdcage trick right here in Cheddarville in 1901."

"Ah, yes. The poster. Come with me." Tip-Toe led the way to the back of the shop. He pointed to a framed poster on the wall. "These were plastered all over town in 1901. This one has hung in each of our family's magic shops. It's our good luck charm." The others crowded around for a close look. Drawings of Houdini, a dove, and a birdcage covered most of the poster. "That must be the Vanishing Birdcage," said Fribble, pointing. "Oh, how I wish I could see that trick." He turned to look at Tip-Toe. "I don't suppose that you do the Vanishing Birdcage trick, do you?"

Tip-Toe smiled at Fribble. "Why, of course."

Fribble's heart skipped a beat. It took him a moment to catch his breath, and then an idea began taking shape. Quickly Fribble explained to Tip-Toe about the school's Fall Festival to be held the following Friday night. He told about the three tricks that he and Tweek would perform, and how Tweek would close their act by playing "Auld Lang Syne" as a tribute to the Great Houdini.

"But it would be really special," Fribble said, "if you came up on stage and did the Vanishing Birdcage." Fribble looked up at the tall elegant mouse, and with nose twitching, asked, "Would you?"

"Why, of course. How could I refuse such an admirer of the Great Houdini," said Tip-Toe. "I would be honored to come to your Fall Festival and perform the Vanishing Birdcage."

Fribble was so thrilled he was in a daze. He stood there, mouth open, unable to talk. But Great Aunt Squeegee thanked the shop owner and then said, "I'd like to buy a little gift for each of these young magicians. Perhaps you'd help select them."

"Of course," said Tip-Toe. "What do you have in mind?"

"I want a magic wand," Scamper said, tugging on his aunt's skirt. "Please. One that I can wave through the air to make things disappear."

Tip-Toe selected a slender little black wand. "It will take a lot of practice before you can make things disappear," he said. "But this is a good wand to start with."

Scamper took the wand and waved it wildly through the air.

"And how about you?" Tip-Toe asked Tweek.

"I really like card tricks," Tweek said.

"Aha!" said Tip-Toe. "Then for you, I'd suggest this book, *Easy Card Tricks,* which comes with a handsome deck of cards." He handed over the boxed set.

"Perfect," Tweek said, and beamed.

"And what about you, my young mouse detective?" said Tip-Toe turning to Fribble.

Before he could open his mouth, Great Aunt Squeegee said, "Oh, I know what he needs, a hat that won't slip down over his eyes."

Tip-Toe took the tall silk hat out of his window and handed it to Fribble. "Let's see if this fits."

Fribble gently took the hat in his paws and put it on his head.

"Looks like a perfect fit," Tip-Toe said, admiring it from all angles.

Fribble stood straight and tall. Then he swept the hat off his head and made a deep bow.

Tip-Toe applauded.

Great Aunt Squeegee paid for their gifts amid squeaks of thanks. They bundled into the car and drove home, dropping Tweek off at his house along the way.

Fribble took his hat box to his room and then came rushing downstairs again. He was so excited that Tip-Toe was going to do the Vanishing Birdcage trick that he simply had to know how it worked. "I need to make a quick trip to the library," he exclaimed to his mother.

"Well, don't be late for dinner," his mother said. "You haven't much time."

"Can I go, too?" asked Scamper.

"Sure," Fribble agreed, and the two hurried down the street.

Miss Scurry greeted them. "Hello, and what are you looking for today?"

"I've checked out your books on magic tricks for kids. They all have the same number, 793.8. But none of them tells about the Vanishing Birdcage. I really want to know how that trick is done. I know it's hard, and I thought it might be in one of the magic books for grown-ups. Do books for grown-ups have the same Dewey decimal numbers as the books for kids?"

"Yes, they do, Fribble. Let me show you where they are." Miss Scurry led the way to the 700s in the adult nonfiction books and located the books on magic tricks. "I think your best bet is to look up 'Vanishing Birdcage' in the index of these books."

"Okay," Fribble said. He took all of the books to a table and began looking up Vanishing Birdcage in each index. But it wasn't listed in any of the books. With a sigh, Fribble returned the books to the shelves, and he and Scamper walked back home.

"Houdini would never explain how he did his tricks," Fribble said. "And I don't think Tip-Toe will tell either, Scamper. So I guess we're going to be as surprised as the rest of the audience when that birdcage vanishes Friday night."

Scamper just smiled and said, "I like surprises."

On the afternoon of the Fall Festival, Fribble and Scamper rushed home from school. Scamper began sniffing loudly the moment he opened the door of the house. A tantalizing aroma was wafting through the air.

"Cake!" he shouted, rushing to the kitchen, where Great Aunt Squeegee was waiting for them.

There on the counter sat a tall cake, iced with pale golden cream cheese. In the center of the cake, made of brightly colored frosting, was a tiny orange carrot with a green stem.

"Carrot cake!" Scamper squeaked. "My favorite."

"It's beautiful!" Fribble said.

"And look!" Scamper pointed to a plate of cupcakes.

"If you check closely, you'll find that one has your name on it," Great Aunt Squeegee said.

Scamper ran for a closer look. Sure enough, one of the cupcakes had "SCAMPER" on it in bright orange. Another, written in green, said "FRIBBLE."

"It's a special snack," Great Aunt Squeegee said.

Fribble and Scamper took their cupcakes over to the kitchen table and gobbled up every delicious crumb along with a glass of milk.

"Now," said Great Aunt Squeegee, chasing them out of the kitchen. "Go and get ready, because we'll leave for the Fall Festival at four o'clock."

That was all the encouragement Fribble and Scamper needed to dash upstairs, wash, and dress. In record time, Fribble put on his suit and top hat and was ready to leave. Now all he had to do was wait impatiently for everyone else.

Fribble's mother almost ran into him in the upstairs hall; he had come to a sudden halt to check the contents of his pockets yet again. "Fribble," she said, "why don't you go down to the living room and read a book? You'll wear a hole in your pockets if you keep pulling your paws in and out of them like that."

Fribble couldn't help it. He had the deck of cards, neatly arranged in one coat pocket, and balloons in the other. The red silk scarf, ping-pong ball, and elastic were tucked in his shirt pocket. He knew where everything was, but he had to keep checking.

Fribble's father was home from work until after Thanksgiving. Great Aunt Squeegee was going to drive Fribble and Scamper to school. Mom and Dad had offered to pick up two friends, Mr. Crumb from across the street and Miss Slippers, who lived above her antique shop just two blocks away.

At four o'clock, Mom and Dad drove off. Great Aunt Squeegee led Fribble and Scamper to her car. She carried the cake. "Scamper, I know you'll hold this cake safely while I drive," Great Aunt Squeegee said. Scamper quickly slid into the front seat, reached for the cake, and held it carefully in both paws. Fribble climbed in the back, and they were off.

In the parking lot, Fribble pressed his nose against the car window. Again he slipped a paw into each coat pocket to check on his magic show supplies.

Great Aunt Squeegee spied a parking place and eased into it. She quickly went around to the side of her car and opened the door. Scamper proudly handed over the precious cake. Then they headed for the front door of the school. They saw Mom, Dad, Miss Slippers, and Mr. Crumb, and quickly joined them.

Dad bought a long strip of twenty-five cent tickets. He tore some off and passed them out to everyone. "Where shall we start?" he asked.

"First, I've got to drop this cake off," said Great Aunt Squeegee.

"And I want to enter the cakewalk and win it!" Scamper said.

The cakewalk, played like musical chairs, was at one end of the cafeteria, so everyone headed there. Great Aunt Squeegee delivered her cake while Fribble and Scamper hurried to get in line to have a turn.

Scritch and Scratch were in charge of the cakewalk this year. Scritch took the tickets and let 24 people come sit in a circle of chairs. When all chairs were filled, Scratch started music on a tape player, and everyone stood and started walking. While they walked in a large circle, Scritch removed two chairs.

Then, when the music stopped, each mouse raced for a chair. The two who didn't find chairs left the circle. This continued until two mice scrambled for the last remaining chair.

Fribble tried the cakewalk and lost twice. Then he left to visit the other booths. But he felt too distracted about the upcoming magic show to take much in. Scamper stayed put at the cakewalk, and on his fourth try, he won! Scratch gave him a winner's button, and Scamper dashed off to claim his prize. Without hesitation, he chose Great Aunt Squeegee's carrot cake. Dad carefully stowed the cake in the trunk of the car.

Everyone had a great time nibbling treats at the food concessions, guessing the weight of a pumpkin or the number of popcorn kernels in a huge jar, admiring the art show, and listening to the storyteller.

At quarter to seven, while the others started for the auditorium to claim good seats for the talent show, Fribble headed backstage. A little shiver of excitement raced down his back. Anxiously, he scanned the crowd. He let out a sigh of relief when he spotted Tip-Toe, taller than everyone else, standing next to Tweek. Tweek clutched the sheet music to "Auld Lang Syne" tightly in his paws. Tip-Toe held something large covered in a black silk cloth. Could it be the birdcage? Fribble's nose twitched as he stared at it. On checking the program, they learned that their act was listed as the Grand Finale.

"That's an honor," Tip-Toe said. "They saved the best for last."

Fribble stroked his whiskers and again frantically fumbled in his pockets.

They stood backstage in the midst of chaos. There were tutus, violins, drum sets, and shouting performers everywhere. And from the auditorium came a steady roar of chatter and laughter.

Finally there were squeaks and whistles as the Master of Ceremonies turned on the microphone. Then a hush descended on both sides of the curtain. Fribble found the sudden quiet more terrifying than the bustle and noise. He trembled.

At last the program began. There were dancers and singers, jump ropers, and instrumentalists.

Tip-Toe looked at the program and whispered to Fribble and Tweek. "There's just one more performance before us. Let's take our places. Everyone ready?"

Fribble felt in his pockets one last time. Carrying his hat, he walked to the edge of the stage, just behind the curtain, and waited. As he caught a glimpse of the enormous crowd, he tried to swallow, but his mouth was dry. What had ever made him think that performing in front of an audience would be fun? He put his tall silk hat firmly on his head and gripped the red scarf tightly in his paw.

The last note of the song died away, and the soloist and her pianist bowed. The Master of Ceremonies went on stage and announced, "For our final number of the evening, Fribble Mouse will present a magic show assisted by Tweek Twitchell on the piano and Tip-Toe Macey from the Abracadabra Magic Shop."

This was it. Fribble's heart was pounding. He strode out onto the middle of the stage and blinked at the bright lights. Thinking of the Great Houdini, Fribble took a deep breath. He whipped the bright red scarf through the air. "Ladies and gentlemen," he cried. "Watch closely as I make this scarf vanish before your very eyes."

Just as he had practiced, Fribble pushed the scarf into his paw which held the hidden ping-pong ball. Then he released the stuffed ball which vanished under his coat, opened his empty paw, and said,

"Shazaam!" His paw was empty and the scarf was gone. Loud applause broke out from the audience.

Fribble motioned toward Tweek, who was still standing backstage. "My assistant will join me for the next piece of magic." Tweek stepped out. Fribble handed him the blue balloon with the yellow one tucked invisibly inside. Tweek blew up the balloons.

"Just a little more air, if you would, my good mouse," Fribble said grandly. And holding tightly to the balloons, Tweek gave another puff.

Smoothly, Fribble waved his paw and pricked the balloon with the pin he had taken from his coat sleeve. "Shazaam!" There was a loud POP! and the blue balloon was suddenly yellow. To more applause, Tweek and Fribble took a bow, then Tweek moved to the piano.

Fribble called a volunteer, Mr. Merriweather Mouse, the mail mouse, from the audience to come up on stage. Fribble said, "Pick a card, remember what it is, then put it with the other cards." Fribble put one paw to his forehead, concentrated, and pretended to read his volunteer's mind. Then he identified the card. Again there was loud applause, and Mr. Merriweather looked surprised that Fribble was right.

"Finally," Fribble said, "I give you that extraordinary magician, from a long line of magicians first trained by the Great Houdini himself, Mr. Tip-Toe Macey, who will perform the famous Vanishing Birdcage. We'll conclude with Tweek playing 'Auld Lang Syne,' the song with which Houdini closed each of his programs."

Tip-Toe came out, bowed, and showed them a gilt cage and a snow white dove. He shut the dove inside the cage, covered it with the silk cloth, and threw the cage high up into the air. It vanished.

For a moment there was a hush, and then thunderous applause. Fribble clapped his paws louder than anyone else. Even though he'd seen the Vanishing Birdcage, he still couldn't believe it. Tip-Toe motioned to Fribble to join him. The two clasped paws, took off their tall silk hats, and bowed, while Tweek played "Auld Lang Syne."

As the curtain closed, Tip-Toe took a moment to congratulate Tweek and Fribble on their great performances. "It's amazing how much you've learned so quickly," Tip-Toe said.

Fribble smiled. It was pretty amazing. It wasn't long ago that he and Scamper had scrubbed clean the marker on the rock in the park and began to

research and uncover its many secrets about the Great Houdini. Fribble wondered what other mysteries were waiting for him.

After the show, Fribble's mother invited Tip-Toe to their house for cake and tea. As they sat happily around the dining table, sipping their tea, Scamper carried in the carrot cake, while Great Aunt Squeegee followed with dessert plates, and Fribble carried the knife.

Handing the long knife to Great Aunt Squeegee, Fribble said, "Shazaam! Let's make this cake disappear!"

And they did.